The KAI STARS of MATARIKI

TUPUĀNUKU and TUPUĀRANGI

Written by
MIRIAMA KAMO

Illustrated by
ZAK WAIPARA

SCHOLASTIC
AUCKLAND SYDNEY NEW YORK LONDON TORONTO
MEXICO CITY NEW DELHI HONG KONG

To our great, great Uncle Wharerau 'Jim' Whaitiri who taught our dad 'Pōua' everything

—MK

In memory of Manawa Ote Rangi Waipara, the guiding star of our whānau mārama

—ZW

First published in 2024 by Scholastic New Zealand Limited
Private Bag 94407, Botany, Auckland 2163, New Zealand

Scholastic Australia Pty Limited
PO Box 579, Gosford, NSW 2250, Australia

ISBN 978-1-77543-869-4

A catalogue record for this book is available from the National Library of New Zealand.

12 11 10 9 8 7 6 5 4 3 2 1 4 5 6 7 8 9 / 2

Illustrations created in watercolours and pencil, and Adobe illustrator using Wacom tablet

Publishing team: Lynette Evans, Penny Scown and Abby Haverkamp
Designer: Smartwork Creative, www.smartworkcreative.co.nz
Typeset in Pangolin Regular
Printed in China by RR Donnelley

Scholastic New Zealand's policy is to use papers that are renewable and made efficiently from wood grown in responsibly managed forests, so as to minimise its environmental footprint.

Have you ever been to Te Mata Hāpuku?
Oh, it's the **best place** in the world!

There are trillions of grey stones, noisy, smashing waves and huge winds. You'll see jagged orange cliffs, lightning fast lizards, and lots of lovely little baches. Some people call it **Birdling's Flat**.

Te Mata Hāpuku is a **magical**, **wild**, **windy** place, famous for its kai, but there are no shops there.

"Who needs shops?" Grandma says. "The kai is all around us!"

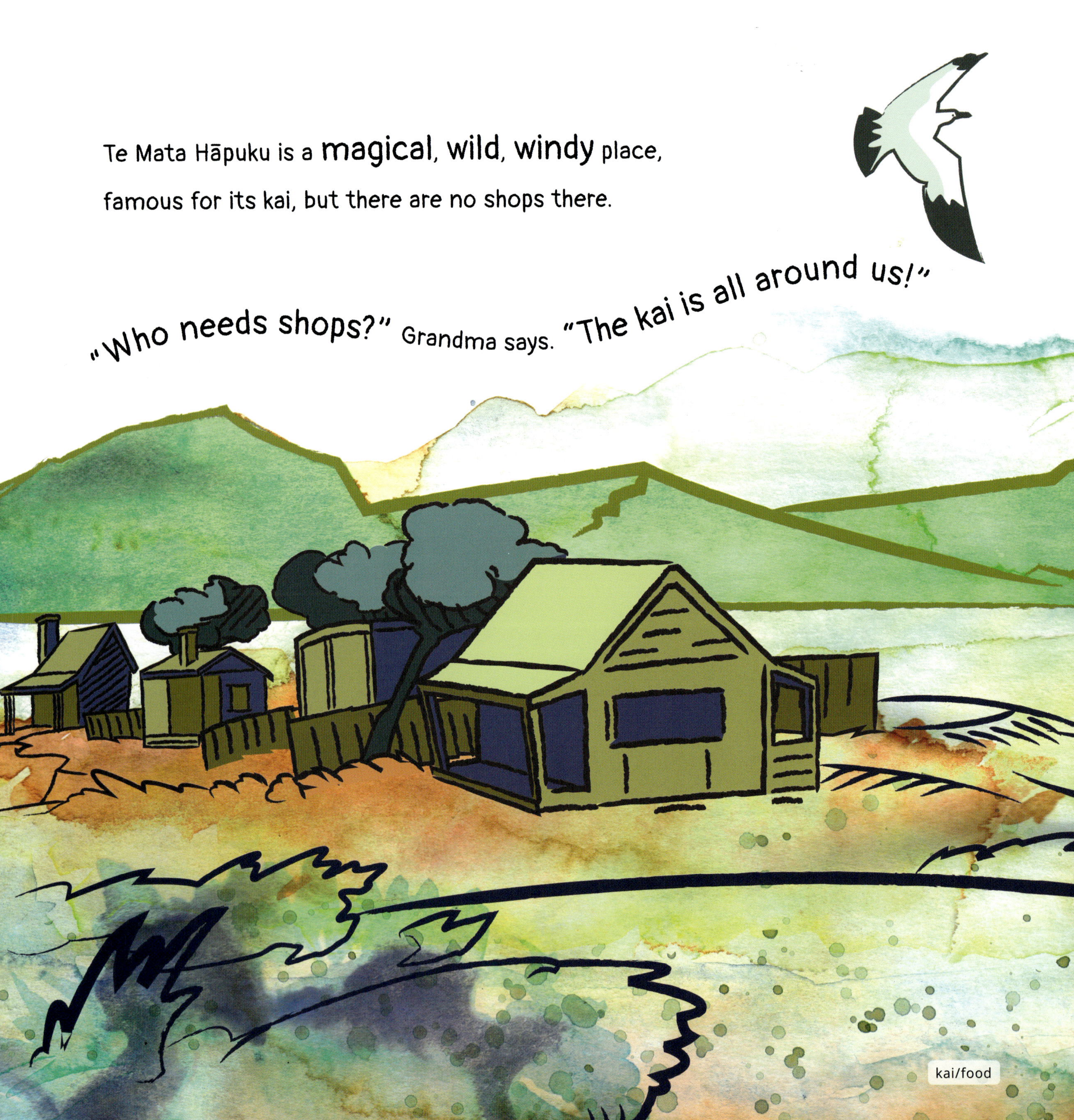

kai/food

Te Rerehua and Sam often visit Grandma and Pōua in their tumbly little house at Te Mata Hāpuku. It's right next to a **big lake** – Te Roto o Wairewa. Even though the lake is shallow and silent, it's very busy beneath the glassy surface.

At night, the children and their grandparents wrap up warmly. Into the **wailing wind** they head, shining torches and **crunching** across stones to the lakeside.

There, beneath the glittering stars, they hook out eels with their gaffs.

Before long, the stony, shallow pit is full of sliding, slippery eels.

The next day, Pōua will hang them in the whata to dry in the wind.

One night, when they went eeling, Grandma, Te Rerehua and Sam lay on the stones looking up at the masses of stars upon stars. Grandma sighed happily. "It'll be a longer night of eeling than usual, tamariki mā. Matariki is just a few months away, so we need to stock up and get ready for our Matariki feast."

"Ooo, a feast!" Te Rerehua exclaimed, her eyes shining. "What's the Matariki feast for?"

tamariki mā/children

"Matariki is when we stop our mahi and focus on whānau," Grandma said. "We plan for the future and give thanks for all our blessings."

"Like chocolate and cake?" suggested Sam.

Grandma laughed. "Kāo. I mean like each other. And we thank the Matariki kai stars. Last Māori New Year we focused on Waitī and Waitā, but this year we're thanking two special stars for all the kai that comes from the earth and the sky."

mahi/work
Kāo/no

"I know who you're talking about," cried Te Rerehua. "The Matariki stars – **Tupuānuku** and **Tupuārangi**."

"**Āe rā!**" replied Grandma. "Tupuānuku tells us about kai that comes from the earth, like kūmara and potatoes – the 'nuku' refers to Papatūānuku. So, who do you think Tupuārangi is named for?"

"Ranginui, the sky father!" shouted both children together.

"Āe, rangi is in the name Tupuārangi. So that means that Tupuārangi tells us about kai that comes from . . .?"

"The sky – like manu, eh Grandma?"

"Āe, and food that grows above the ground, like fruit on trees."

manu/birds

"Last Matariki," Grandma continued, "both stars were bright in the sky, meaning we'd have lots of ika. And just look how many **tuna** we have!"

ika/fish
tuna/eels

The pit was full of big, squirming, snakelike eels.

"Kua oti tā tātou mahi ināianei," called Pōua.

"Our work's finished now, let's go home!"

The months flew by, and soon enough it was Matariki. The star cluster hung high and clear in the sky.

The children were **so excited**.

The eels had been dried and frozen and were ready to be cooked in the umu. The Matariki feast for the people of Te Mata Hāpuku was the very next day. Grandma knew the people would bring mountains of vegetables and juicy fruits fresh from their gardens to honour Tupuānuku and Tupuārangi.

As the day was closing and shadows crept up the stony beach, Pōua and Grandma settled in for an early night, and the children went for a walk to the lake.

umu/earth oven

"I'm so happy," said Te Rerehua, hugging herself.

"Me too", agreed Sam. "Tomorrow's the big day. But wait, what's that noise?"

The children heard funny, slurping, burping noises.

SHLU-U-R-RP . . .

CRUNCH,

CRUNCH . . . MUNCH!

Peering around a mingimingi bush, the children saw a very happy group of patupaiarehe down by the lakeside. They were eating eels, the juices running down their glowing white faces.

"Yum!"

cried one, its flame-coloured hair flying in the wind.

"This is the best!"

"Hey!" yelled Sam, jumping out.

"Where did you get that tuna?"

The patupaiarehe grinned wickedly.

"We stole it from Pōua and Grandma."

Te Rerehua and Sam were alarmed.

"Wait . . . how much is left?"

With a final SCHMACK, SCHLURP and BURRRRP, the tiniest patupaiarehe announced, "Karekau!"

"None!" cried Te Rerehua. "E hika, why did you do that?"

"We hate cooked kai," the patupaiarehe continued, "and they were going to ruin this tuna by cooking it in the umu. So we saved it!"

Karekau/none
E hika/My goodness

"Oh no!" cried Sam.

"It was meant for our Matariki feast tomorrow.

What will we serve now?"

"Not our problem," said the grinning patupaiarehe.

"Āe rā, yes it is," said Te Rerehua. She grabbed two patupaiarehe, and marched them to the lake. "You'll have to catch some more!"

Sam grabbed two patupaiarehe as well and followed his sister.

"But it's too late in the season for eels," they protested. "They don't run at Matariki."

Sam and Te Rerehua thought for a moment. One thing that patupaiarehe hate more than cooked food is sunlight. It burns their delicate white skin.

"Grandma says this lake is full of ika," said Sam. "Get fishing! Or we'll keep you here until the sun comes up."

All night long, the naughty patupaiarehe fished, pulling in piles of big, fat fish in their special raupō nets. By dawn, their sacks were full.

The children hauled the ika home to Grandma and Pōua and explained what had happened.

"How will we make sure they don't come and steal it back later?"

Grandma mused, looking at Pōua.

"If patupaiarehe don't like cooked food," Pōua said, "we'd better get cooking."

Before long, the umu was steaming with kai: the ika, and baskets of **kūmara**, **cabbage** and **carrots**. Pōua and Grandma also prepared corn fritters, swan eggs, steamed pudding and sea tulips called kaeo.

The people of Te Mata Hāpuku brought piles of vegetables: stuffed kūmara, steamed kamokamo and wilted watercress. There were bowls of crisp apples and juicy pears.

If the villagers had looked to the shadows in the distance, they might have seen cross little white faces glaring at them. But they were too happy to notice. They ate and laughed and chatted and planned.

As the stars grew **brighter** in the evening, they sang and shared Matariki stories.

Te Rerehua and Sam were happy,
i te tino harikoa rāua. They looked
to the night sky where Tupuānuku
and Tupuārangi twinkled happily.
It was the best Matariki ever.